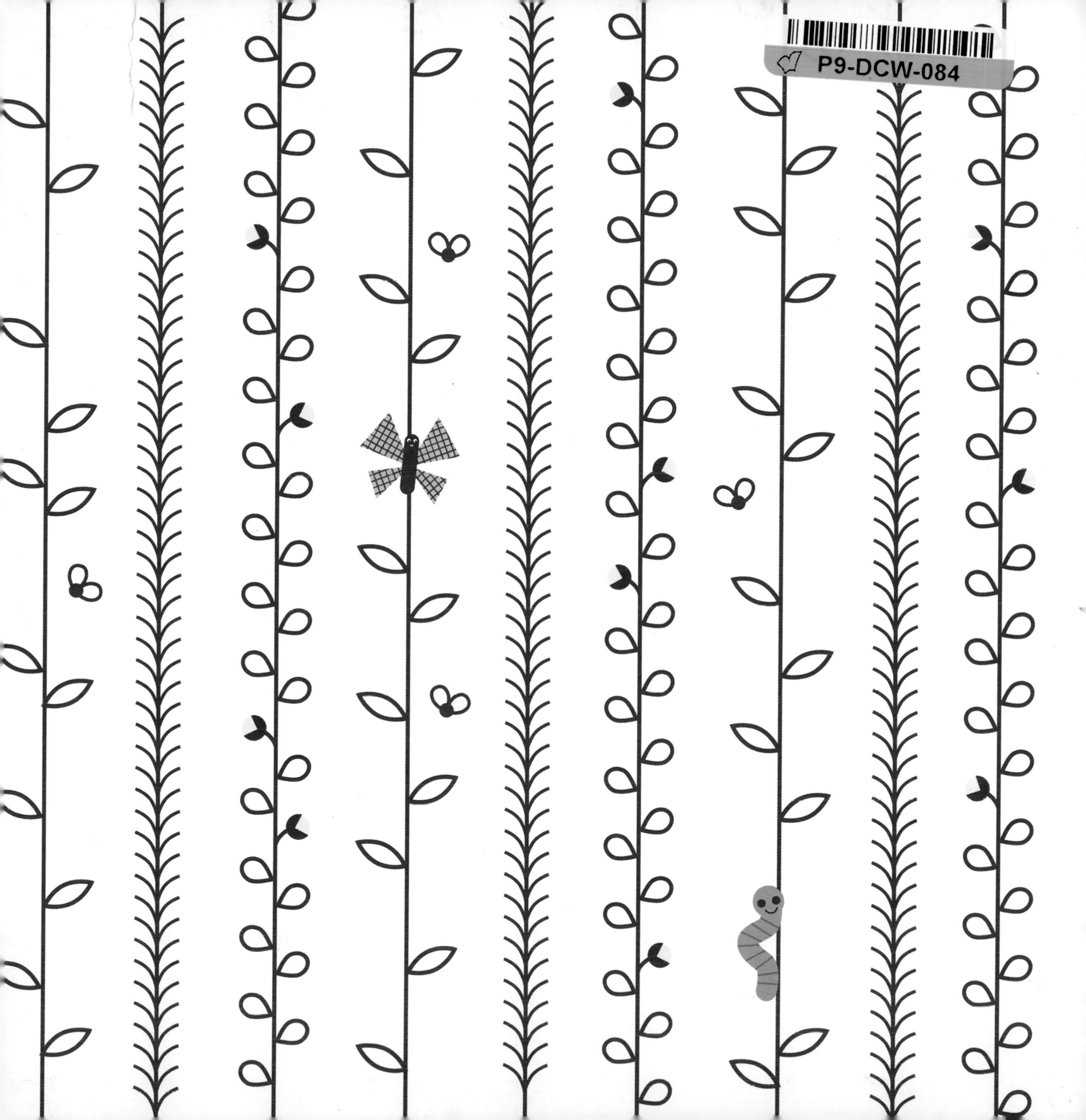

For Riley:
A fine farmer, and friend
—S. G.

All rights reserved. Published in the United States by Random House Children's Books,
a division of Random House LLC, a Penguin Random House Company, New York.

Random House and the colophon are registered trademarks of Random House LLC.

Visit us on the Web! randomhousekids.com

Educators and librarians, for a variety of teaching tools, visit us at
RHTeachersLibrarians.com

Library of Congress Cataloging-in-Publication Data
Gillingham, Sara, author, illustrator.
How to grow a friend / Sara Gillingham. — First edition.
pages cm.
Summary: "Friendship advice given as gardening tips." —Provided by publisher.
ISBN 978-0-385-37669-3 (trade) — ISBN 978-0-375-97325-3 (lib. bdg.) — ISBN 978-0-375-98216-3 (ebook)
[1. Friendship—Fiction.] I. Title.
PZ7.G41554Ho 2013 [E]—dc23 2013008885

Book design by John Sazaklis

MANUFACTURED IN CHINA

10 9 8 7 6 5 4 3 2 1

First Edition

How to Grow a Friend

by Sara Gillingham

Random House New York

To grow a friend,

first plant a seed in good soil.

A friend needs water . . .

warm sunshine . . .

and space to bloom.

To grow a friend, talk

and listen.

It doesn't happen
overnight.

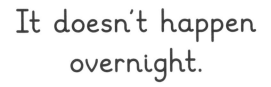

Sometimes a friend bugs you.

To grow a friend,

chase the bugs away
together!

And don't let your friend
get stuck in the weeds.

If a friend is drooping,

do something sweet.

Good friends stand by each other in rain

or shine.

Good friends
make things brighter.

To grow a garden of friends,

remember that new buds can sprout . . .

in surprising places!

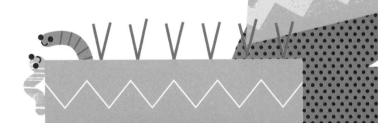

And there is always room
for one more.

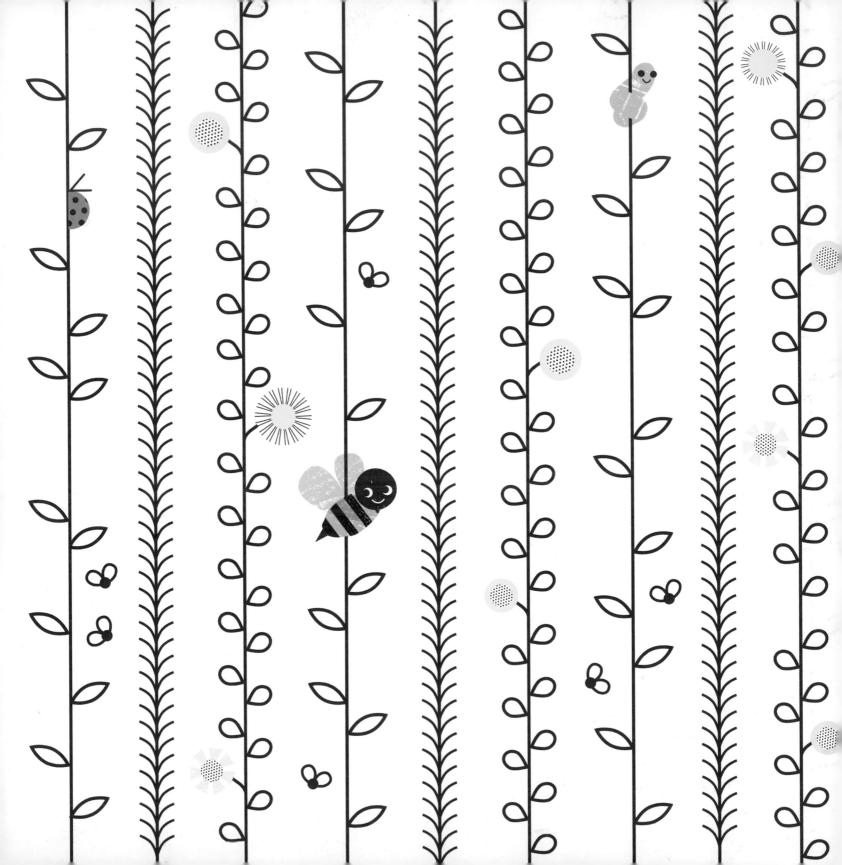